Memories That Bless and Burn

A Novel

Robert Hamblin

for
Ann and Dale Abadie
and
Gerald and Julie Walton

who stayed

O' memories that bless and burn
O' barren gain and bitter loss

Memories That Bless and Burn

ONE

He had not been back to the old home place in more than twenty years. He had thought he would never come back, but lately he had been feeling a strong impulse to return. He knew nothing would be the same, but perhaps that would make it easier for him to make the visit.

He still owned the forty-acre farm that had belonged to his parents and where he had grown up. His last trip there had been to attend the joint funeral of his parents, who had died in an automobile accident, driving home from Tupelo on a rainy night.

Randy didn't really know why he had kept the farm all these years, since farm life was another thing from his youth that he was happy to leave behind. Early on he had leased the crop land, about thirty acres, to a neighboring farmer. In recent years the lease had been assigned to a corporation headquartered in Birmingham that had bought or leased several of the area farms and converted them into a large beef cattle operation. Most of the forty acres he owned were now part of the fenced-in pasture for a herd of white-faced cattle. The small farms that he knew as a boy were largely a thing of the past. And cotton was no longer king, except down in the Delta. In north Mississippi now the principal crops were soybeans, corn, and hay.

He had booked a room in the Holiday Express in Blyden, about ten miles from the New Harmony community where the home place was located. Yesterday he drove around the old neighborhood to see how things had changed, and he was even more shocked than he expected to be.

In his boyhood there were only two brick buildings in the community—the home belonging to Bryson Craig, the area's mail carrier, and the Baptist church. Now they were the only structures of those he remembered still standing. All the others—small frame houses, sharecroppers' shotgun shanties, barns and other outbuildings— were no longer here. A few newer homes, some quite large, were scattered throughout the area, inhabited, Randy suspected, by people who worked in town.

On his way back to town he visited the church cemetery to view the graves of his parents. He stood briefly in front of the single stone, reading the words: "John Alfred Morris / September 21, 1917 – May 6, 1970" and "Anna Elizabeth Morris / February 16, 1918 –

May 6, 1970." He didn't speak. What more is to be said, he thought.

Returning to New Harmony today, he had a specific task in mind. He parked his car in what used to be the front yard of the farm house he lived in. He slowly walked the grounds, remembering each room of the house—his that was called "the south room," his parents' bedroom, the living room with the black-and-white TV, the dining room, and the kitchen. He stood quietly for a moment, waiting to see if the sound of his parents' voices would float back into his memory. They didn't, so he moved on.

At the back of the lot he passed the location of the outhouse, expecting its foul stench still to rise from the ground, and walked on to where the smokehouse, small barn, and tool shed had stood. When he was a very small boy, his father plowed his crops with mules; but later he bought a two-row

Allis Chalmers tractor. Randy had learned to drive that tractor before he could drive a car.

Encountering no ghosts except those of his own imagination, he returned to the car. He opened the back door and removed a shovel he had placed between the seats. Then he walked back across the vacant lot and entered the large patch of woods that stood on the western edge of the property. Continuing deeper into the woods, he noticed the stumps and new growth resulting from a thinning of the timber he had allowed a local logging company to perform a few years ago. Mostly what were left were worthless scrub oak, blackjack, sassafras, and persimmon. Now he regretted the loss of the tall oaks and hickories and gums, but at the time he didn't think he would ever return, so he approved the harvest and pocketed the check.

He walked deeper into the woods. He was surprised to find that the tree he was looking for was still there.

It was a tall sycamore that stood at the edge of a small creek that flowed through the property. He located a spot on the north side of the tree, not far from its base, and started digging. Since the tree had grown over the intervening years, he couldn't be sure of the exact spot; but what he was looking for had not been buried very deeply, so it shouldn't take him very long to complete his search.

He measured out an area about six feet wide and dug to a depth of six-to-ten inches. Fifteen minutes into his dig he heard the shovel strike metal—the sound he was listening for. Focusing on that spot, he kept digging until he unearthed a small metal box, in actuality a discarded tool box that had once belonged to his father.

It had been buried there beneath the sycamore almost forty years earlier, by three ten-year-old playmates who roamed these woods playing their childhood games. They had filled the box with various items they had selected and buried it as a time capsule, agreeing to meet back at the spot on the Fourth of July in the year they turned twenty-one, 1965, dig up the box, and reminisce about their childhood adventures. Sadly, however, circumstances had prevented that reunion from taking place.

And one of those circumstances was the reason he did not visit one particular location in his favorite woods on this day of his return. He didn't know when, if ever, he would be able to go there.

"The Three Musketeers," as the boys called themselves, were Billy Ray White, Sylvester Johnson, and Randy Morris. Billy Ray and Randy were white; Sylvester, or Syl, was black. They each belonged to a farm family: Billy Ray's father owned a farm just down the road from the Morris farm; Syl's daddy was a sharecropper for Mr. Morris.

The boys' feet had touched every square foot of these woods, as on Saturdays and summer days, freed from the burden of schoolwork, they romped and played their imaginary games. They were pirates, climbing the trees to look for rival ships. They were cowboys, hiding behind the trees and firing their cap pistols at outlaws or Indians who were threatening the town. They were soldiers, always Confederates, reprising the Civil War battle that was fought on this very ground almost a century earlier.

When they tired of playing their games, the boys strolled through the woods with their b-b guns, pestering squirrels and rabbits and shooting at and sometimes killing blue jays and crows. Syl did not own a b-b gun, but he was allowed to take turns with Billy Ray's and Randy's. At Syl's insistence, the boys never shot at robins or songbirds.

"You'll have bad luck if you shoot a songbird," Syl said, and Billy Ray and Randy believed him.

After rains, the boys scoured the washed-out gullies for arrowheads or an occasional grapeshot or Minié ball left there from the battle.

The boys had other friends in the New Harmony community—Bobby Russell, whose parents owned the general store, Gerald, Jimmy, Hugh, Sonny, even a couple of girls, one of whom, Becky, could hit a baseball farther than any of the boys. Together they all played baseball games in Willie Quinn's pasture, or basketball games on the basket nailed to the side of Jess Haygood's barn.

But none of these other friends was invited to join them in the woods. That was their own private space, reserved for them alone—the Three Musketeers. There they spent many carefree days, not yet aware of the gloom and tragedy that was about to descend upon their lives.

The lock and hinges were rusted shut, so Randy would need some tools to open the box. Back in Blyden, he stopped at a garage and asked the mechanic if he could borrow a screwdriver and a hammer.

"Looks like you found some buried treasure," the mechanic said. He was an older man, maybe sixty or sixty-five.

"Yeah, I hope so," Randy replied.

"Say, you look familiar. Do I know you?" the man asked.

"I'm Randy Morris. I grew up out at New Harmony. But I haven't been back here for quite a while."

"Morris," the man said. "I remember some Morrises. They were killed in an automobile wreck, as I recall."

"Yes, my parents, John and Anna Morris," Randy said.

"Sorry for your loss. I'm Wilson Bryant." He extended his hand.

"I heard you became a lawyer," he continued. "Is that right?"

"That's right," Randy said, shaking the man's hand. "I now live in St. Louis."

"Well, welcome home. Let's see if we can get that box opened."

It took a few tries, but with the hammer and the screwdriver Randy was able to pry the lid open.

He scraped the dirt and debris from the box and placed it, the contents unexamined, back in the car. He didn't want company as he reviewed what was inside.

"Many thanks," he said, as he climbed back into the car and drove away.

In the motel parking lot he opened the box and looked inside. There was a copy of the *Tupelo Daily Journal*, dated July 12, 1954, wrapped in plastic. The paper was faded brown, but still intact, still legible. The lead story treated the organization of the White Citizens' Council in Indianola, Mississippi. Another story announced President Eisenhower's plan to create a national interstate highway system.

There was also a cowboy card, slightly water-damaged, with a photo of Gene

Autry, a legacy of the many Saturdays
Randy had sat in the Ritz Theater in
Blyden and watched western matinees
starring Autry, Roy Rogers, Hopalong
Cassidy, Lash Larue, Randolph Scott, Bob
Steele, and others. Randy collected
cowboy cards the way some of his
friends collected baseball cards.

Continuing to look through the items,
he found objects that each of the boys
had contributed to the collection:
arrowheads and Minié balls, unusually
shaped rocks and stones, even fossils
and seashells that Randy learned later in
school were residue from prehistoric
times when the area had been under
water, a part of the vast gulf that
covered most of the North American
continent. There was also a Kodak
snapshot that Randy's mother had made
of the three boys. They were dressed in
ragged overalls, and each was smiling,
their arms draped around each other's

shoulders, seemingly without a care in the world. They looked like they would be friends for life.

One item brought tears to Randy's eyes. It was Syl's rabbit foot, his good luck charm. Syl's whole family had been very superstitious, and Syl was always looking for talismans to hold bad luck at bay. But he hadn't succeeded. Maybe if he had kept this rabbit foot he could have avoided his terrible fate.

Randy saw no evidence that the box had been opened before now. He had often wondered, with Syl gone, whether Billy Ray had ever found his way back to the spot. But apparently he had not. Now both he and Syl were dead, and it was left to Randy, here in middle age, to see if he could find some sense and purpose in their story. Thus far he had been unable to do so. But maybe that was why he had come back home.

The next day Randy dropped by Martin's Hardware Store in Blyden. The lettering on the sign across the front of the two-story brick building, though now quite faded, was still legible. It was the one he remembered from his boyhood: "Martin's Hardware / Doing Business in Blyden Since 1934."

Entering the store, Randy asked the clerk if he might see Mr. Martin. "He's in his office," the clerk said, pointing to the rear of the store. "Go right on back."

The man seated at the desk in the office was not the one Randy expected to see. This one was much too young.

"My name is Randy Morris. I was looking for Travis Martin," Randy explained.

"That's my dad," the man said, rising from his chair to shake Randy's hand. "I'm Todd Martin. I now run the store."

"Glad to see it's still in the family," Randy said.

"Third generation," Todd said. "We're still hanging on. Don't know how much longer we'll be able to hold off the large chain stores, but so far we're managing to do so."

"I remember your father from the time I was a boy growing up in the New Harmony community," Randy said. "My father was a farmer. He used to do business here."

"That was before my time," Todd said. "But I'm sure my dad would remember your family."

"I was wondering if he might be able to give me some information about some people I'm hoping to locate— Robert and Clara Johnson. They were sharecroppers on my dad's farm."

"I don't recognize the names," Todd said. "But Daddy would probably remember, and I'm sure he'd be happy to meet with you. He's in his eighties now and seldom comes to the store anymore, but he's in good health and I know he'd welcome a visit from you. He likes company."

"I'd appreciate that," Randy said.

"He lives just south of town, on Highway 45. I'll give you directions to the address, and I'll call to let him know you're coming by for a visit."

"Many thanks," Randy said, reaching to shake hands again.

Driving down Highway 45, just below the Blyden city limits, Randy saw the sign that read: "Billy Ray White Memorial Highway."

When Randy arrived at the address given him, Mr. Martin was seated in a rocking chair on the front porch, waiting to greet his visitor.

"Randy Morris," he said, as Randy climbed the steps onto the porch. "You look just like your daddy. I remember when you used to come with him to the hardware store."

He shook Randy's hand and motioned to the other huge rocker on the porch. "Come in and have a seat."

"Thanks for seeing me," Randy said. "Good to see you're in such good health."

"I've been blessed," Mr. Martin said. "I could still take care of the store, but it was time to let Todd take over. So I retired two years ago."

"So sorry about your parents," he continued. "That was such a tragic accident."

"Yes, thank you," Randy said.

Always, when there was any mention of his parents' death, he remembered that his father had poor eyesight and had trouble driving. Once, when Randy was just a teenager and had just gotten his driver's license, he was riding with his dad when a rainstorm came up. His father pulled to the side of the road and asked Randy to drive on home. Randy had already left the state when his parents died, but had he been there, he would always think, he could have driven his parents to the doctor's office that day. Another of the many what if's in Randy's life.

"That was always a dangerous stretch of road," Mr. Martin said. "Especially in bad weather. Lots of traffic, and just two lanes. It's four lanes now, as you see."

"Yes, I noticed. Just one of many changes in the area, I see."

"You became a lawyer, I understand, and moved up north," Mr. Martin said. "Your parents were very proud of you."

"Well, I don't think I became the kind of lawyer Daddy would have preferred, but we have to make our own choices."

"What brings you back to this part of the world?" Mr. Martin asked. "We haven't seen you around here for quite a while."

"I'm tying up some loose ends," Randy said. "I still own the family farm and need to decide what to do with it. And I was hoping to contact a family that sharecropped with Daddy—Robert and Clara Johnson, if they're still alive. I wonder if you remember them. Everybody in the county came to your store at one time or another."

"Yes, I remember Robert and Clara. A n----r couple, right?"

"Yes," Randy said, "they're black."

"I don't think they live around here anymore," Mr. Martin said. "I seem to recall that maybe they moved to Corinth. Sorry, I just don't know."

"Well, thanks for your time," Randy said. "Good to see you again."

As Randy was leaving, Mr. Martin said, "Say, didn't the Johnsons have that

boy that was paralyzed in an accident
out there on the farm?"

"Yes," Randy said. "Sylvester."

Randy went to visit Roger Magee, a
high school classmate and football
teammate. They sat in the den of the
Magees' colonial style house in the
nicest residential section of town,
sipping iced tea and talking about old
times.

Roger had coached football for a few
years and then got into the insurance
business. A huge man, even in middle
age he looked like he could still hold his
own as an offensive tackle. Randy had
followed his blocks many times for gains
against opposing teams. The Blyden
Bearcats traditionally had good football
teams, though they could seldom beat
their archrival, Pierce City.

Roger had been very successful as an insurance salesman, and he and Randy had stayed in touch over the years with occasional letters and phone calls. But this was the first time they had seen each other since the funeral of Randy's parents.

"Long time no see," Roger said. "But I hear you're still out there trying to save the world."

"Doing my best," Randy said. "But sometimes I think the world is past saving."

"Well, maybe Mississippi isn't so different from the rest of the world after all," Roger said. "We could sure use a little saving around here. There was a time, with Governor Winter, when it looked like Mississippi was coming out of the Dark Ages. But that didn't last."

The men talked on, about their high school days, their mutual friends and teammates, Coach Claiborne.

"He was a bear," Roger said. "I sure don't miss those two-a-days in that sweltering August heat. He died just last year, you know."

"Yes, I heard." Randy still subscribed to the *Blyden News*, the town's weekly paper, so he had kept up with local happenings.

"You were a good running back," Roger said. "I always thought you should have been All-Conference."

"I had my moments," Randy said "You guys up front made my job a lot easier. And I was small. I didn't need a big hole to run through."

"Well, you ran through a bunch of them."

"I see where Billy Ray has a highway named after him," Randy said.

"Yeah, he was chairman of the House Financial Committee and he funneled a lot of money into this part of the state. For roads, schools, that furniture factory north of town. And he was so . . . what's the word, charismatic? You'll recall that he was elected to the legislature when he was twenty-five, and I think he could have held the office as long as he wanted it. There was even talk that he might run for governor."

"Heart attack, I heard," Randy said.

"Yes, he was only forty-five. Quite a shock. Got my attention. I went on a diet for a month and even pulled out my exercise bike from the garage."

"I guess he never changed his mind politically?" Randy said.

"Oh, no," Roger said. "He knew which side his bread was buttered on. Right-wing Republican all the way."

"And racist," Randy said. "I saw that when we were together at Ole Miss."

"The Solid South still," Roger said. "But now Solid red. That's what integration did to the South. Made all the Roosevelt Democrats into Goldwater Republicans. Including Billy Ray."

"How do you get away with your liberal views?" Randy asked. "Judging by this house, they don't seem to hurt you financially."

"The bank still owns a part of the house," Roger said, laughing, "but I don't let politics interfere with my business. I'm a closet liberal, I'm afraid. Of course, I can be honest with you. You're not a client."

"What do you hear from our other classmates?" Randy asked.

"Not much. Not many of them stayed here. Several of them moved to Memphis. Some, like you, moved even farther away. But Mary Jo has just moved back here. Y'all dated some in high school, didn't you?"

"Yeah, a few times. It never became serious."

Mary Jo Abbott was the school beauty, cheerleader and Homecoming queen, one of the most popular girls at Blyden High.

"Well, she's divorced her husband and come back to town. Give her a call. You're divorced, too, right?"

They talked on a while longer, recalling their shared experiences.

"You wouldn't know where Robert and Clara Johnson might be, would you?" Randy asked. "They were sharecroppers on our farm. I've been trying to get in touch with them."

"No. I remember them, but I don't know where they are now."

Randy decided to return the time capsule to its place of burial. So he drove back to New Harmony and, box and shovel in hand, walked through the woods to the spot. He had placed all of the original items back in the box—and added one more. It was the June 3, 1992 issue of the *Blyden News.*

It was a gorgeous summer day. The sunlight filtering through the lattices of the limbs and leaves performed a moving light show on the ground. A mild breeze, cooled by the shade of the trees, danced across his skin.

In college, in Dr. Harriman's lit class, he had read William Faulkner's story "The Bear." He never finished the two or three Faulkner novels he tried to read, but he loved "The Bear." Ike McCaslin's woods reminded him of his own. His were not as big, and they housed no bears or deer, but they created in him the same sense of a magical, sacred place.

He sat down and leaned his back against the sycamore. He could hear the soft trickle of the creek flowing nearby and the sweet chatter of the songbirds flitting from tree to tree. He closed his eyes and called forth the memory of the time he spent here as a boy, often with Billy Ray and Syl but sometimes when he just wanted to be alone. He had never found another place in which he felt so at peace.

Breaking the reverie and returning to the task at hand, he buried the tool box again in the earth and packed and smoothed the ground all around. Then he headed for another spot in the woods.

He hadn't intended to go there when he entered the woods, in fact, had always assumed that he would probably never go there again. But now a sudden and urgent compulsion drove him to visit the place. He propped the shovel against the sycamore and headed deeper into the trees.

The location was at the far edge of the woods at the top of a steep incline that fell away sharply to the open field below. The area was all covered over now with sumac, pokeweed, and other wild growth, but once it had been a smooth pathway—for a sled during the infrequent snow-and-ice storms that came during north Mississippi winters, and a raceway for the homemade cart the Three Musketeers built the summer when they were eleven.

They spent much of that summer assembling the cart. They searched throughout the community for parts. All the neighbors cooperated. For their front wheels they used two wheels off a rusted-out child's wagon they found in Mr. Palmer's tool shed. For the back wheels they used the ones from an old, discarded bicycle. They used broom and mop handles for the axles. They nailed together a small, flat bed for the cart out of odd pieces of lumber they found in Billy Ray's dad's workshop. They tied the whole contraption together with baling wire.

They cleared weeds and undergrowth and leveled the dirt to construct a ramp on the steep slope. Once the ramp was finished, the boys were ready for their big adventure. They took turns riding the cart down the incline, holding on tightly until it came to a stop at the foot of the hill. The cart had no steering mechanism, but the boys learned that they could maintain a degree of control over their direction by leaning their weight from one side to the other. It was all grand fun.

It was the third day of the thrills and excitement of riding the cart down the hill, the boys feeling their heart race as the cart picked up speed, the wind fanning their faces, their loud laughter and raucous screams of joy echoing off the trunks of trees. Time and time again, one after the other, they climbed onto the cart and delighted in its breathtaking rush down the hill.

Now today, these many years later, Randy stood at the top of the hill and watched it all happen again in his mind's eye.

It was Syl's turn. He flashed that huge smile at Randy and Billy Ray, climbed onto the cart, and waited, excitedly, for them to give the cart a big push. Then he was off again, sailing down the hill.

But he never reached the end of the path. Halfway down the hill one of the front wheels flew off the cart, and the vehicle tumbled on end over end. Syl was thrown from the wreck, his head striking the base of a small tree. Randy and Billy Ray stood, terrified, at the top of the hill, waiting for Syl to climb to his feet. But he never moved.

TWO

When Randy graduated from Blyden High School in May 1961, he wasn't sure what he wanted to do with his life. He knew he didn't want to remain on the farm, and he was fairly sure he didn't want to live in Blyden the rest of his life. Maybe college would help him make up his mind. He had applied to enroll at Ole Miss in the fall. One reason he chose Ole Miss was that three or four of his high school classmates had decided to enroll there. One of those was Billy Ray.

No one in Randy's family had gone to college. But his favorite teacher, Mrs. Stanley, his history teacher, had encouraged him to consider doing so. He made good grades, had a curious mind, and paid close attention the day she told the class, "You can make a living with your hands or with your minds. Consider doing the latter."

Randy had fallen in love with reading in the fifth grade, when another teacher, Mrs. Ratliff, encouraged her pupils to check out books from the small library she housed in bookcases at the back of her classroom. Almost every Friday throughout the whole school year, Randy would check out a book for the weekend—usually a Zane Grey western or a story about the Lone Ranger or Gene Autry, since this was the phase of his life when he was obsessed with cowboys.

Later, in the seventh grade, he read his first classical novel—*Les Miserables* by Victor Hugo. He also developed an interest in biography, enjoying reading about the lives of George Washington, Abraham Lincoln, and other important historical figures. In high school he was one of the few students who didn't complain about being asked to read *Julius Caesar* and *Macbeth*.

He didn't care much for science or mathematics, but he loved history and literature. He wasn't sure which he liked best, but when he was asked to declare a major at Ole Miss, he listed history.

As chance would have it, Randy's sophomore year at Ole Miss happened to be the year that James Meredith enrolled in the university. The first African-American student in the school, Meredith was a 29-year-old Air Force veteran who had already completed three years of college. He had first sought entrance to Ole Miss eighteen months earlier, but was denied entrance, as the U.S. Court of Appeals later concluded, "solely because he was a Negro." Only after an exhaustive court battle which led to contempt citations against a number of state officials and university administrators was the university compelled to admit Meredith.

Just a week before classes were scheduled to begin, as Randy was packing up to move back to the campus after spending the summer at home helping out on the farm, Billy Ray dropped by Randy's house for a visit.

"Looks like we're gonna have a n----r classmate this year," he said.

"Maybe so," Randy replied. "That's what a lot of people say."

"Don't you believe it," Randy's father interjected. "Governor Barnett will take care of that n----r. He'll be declared insane, like the others, and sent to an asylum until he comes to his senses. Hell, he is insane. Any sane n----r wouldn't want to go to school with white folks."

"Bilbo was right," his father continued. "If the n----rs are allowed to go to school with whites and sit with them and eat with them, next thing you know they'll be dating one another and getting married. The old saying is correct: give 'em an inch and they'll take a mile. Miscegenation is a bigger threat to our way of life than the atomic bomb."

Randy said nothing when his father let go with such pronouncements, but he had become increasingly uncomfortable with such sentiments. For one thing, such attitudes seemed not at all to square with Randy's own personal experience—or his father's either, if his father were only honest enough to admit it. His father had always had friendly relationships with the black sharecroppers who lived on their place. Syl Johnson, the son of one of those sharecroppers, had been one of Randy's best boyhood playmates, almost a brother; and Syl's mother, Clara, had always been close to Randy's mother. Clara helped his mother wash clothes in the huge iron pot in the back yard, stoking the fire, stirring the clothes with a broom handle, and hanging them out to dry. Clara also helped out at hog killing time, she and his mother grinding the sausage and cooking out the lard and cracklings after the men had killed and gutted and carved the animal. Randy had seen the two women many times seated at their kitchen table, drinking a cup of coffee and just talking, like friends of whatever color are inclined to do.

Randy had not yet made up his mind about integration; in fact, like most Mississippians, white and black, he had tried to ignore the whole issue and tend to his own business. But it was becoming more and more difficult to deny that old attitudes and behavior were under fierce attack. And extremists on both sides of the issue were becoming more and more vocal and, in some cases, violent. His father was one of those extremists—a rabid Dixiecrat and, as such, a big supporter of Governor Barnett and the White Citizens' Council, the state-based organization whose goal was to resist federal pressure and maintain the age-old condition of white supremacy masked as states' rights.

Along with other Ole Miss students that fateful September, Randy followed the developments as day after day Meredith, accompanied by lawyers and a host of federal marshals, sought to register for classes, only to be turned away time and again. Three weeks into the semester, as Governor Barnett continued to defy federal mandates and refuse Meredith admission, crowds of segregationists and white supremacists descended upon Oxford.

On Sunday afternoon, September 30, Randy was seated with a group of students in the dorm lounge, watching a baseball game on TV. Suddenly another student burst into the room.

"All hell's breaking loose in the Circle!" he shouted. "C'mon, guys, let's go!"

Curious, Randy joined the group of several students who left the dormitory and walked to the Circle, the university's spacious lawn that fronted the Lyceum, to see what was going on.

The crowd, which had been flowing into Oxford for the last few days, some from as far away as Texas and Georgia, had now grown to several hundred in size and was congregated in the vicinity of the monument of the Confederate soldier. Visible on the opposite side of the Circle were armed federal marshals ringing the Lyceum, where it was presumed that Meredith at some point would be registered for classes.

Many students, Randy included, milled freely about the area, mixing with the crowd, talking to the protestors, listening to what was being said. The crowd was vocal and agitated, but not yet violent.

"Where you guys from?" Randy heard someone ask one of the protestors.

"We're from Birmin'ham," the man said. "We come to hep yo' guvnor."

"But he said to do it peacefully," the questioner said.

"Yeah, but we know what he meant, don't we," the man said.

Throughout the afternoon and early evening the protestors had been content to spout segregationist slogans and hurl verbal insults at the marshals. But with the arrival of darkness the crowd became more aggressive, and violence erupted. Randy watched as the mob pelted the marshals with bricks, lead pipes, bottles, and Molotov cocktails, then quickly retreated as the marshals responded by firing canisters of tear gas into the crowd. Randy could hear sporadic gunfire throughout the area.

Around 9 p.m. Randy saw a tall, slender man climb onto the base of the Confederate monument and address the crowd.

"You've been betrayed!" the man shouted to the mob. "You've been betrayed! Don't let them do this to you! Fight back!"

Randy watched as another man, wearing a clerical collar, climbed up on the monument beside the speaker and started talking with him, obviously trying to persuade the man to desist and come down. But the man pushed the minister away, and then hands reached up from the crowd below, roughly pulling the minister to the ground.

"You've been betrayed!" the speaker resumed.

The crowd now started to move en masse toward the Lyceum. There was more gunfire. Randy watched as vehicles belonging to news agencies and TV crews were overturned and set ablaze. More Molotov cocktails were thrown in the direction of the marshals, exploding when they hit the ground and setting the grass on fire. Randy retreated from the war zone, taking a position of relative safety across University Avenue but from where he could still witness the action.

Next Randy watched as a parade of Mississippi Highway Patrol cars passed along University Avenue, bumper to bumper, not headed in the direction of the Lyceum and the marshals as one would expect, but going in the opposite direction, leaving the campus. A patrolman driving one of the vehicles leaned out the window and shouted to the mob, "Kill the son of a bitch!"

Not far from where Randy was standing was the construction site for a new science building going up on campus. Randy watched as numerous rioters, including several students he recognized, visited the site to pick up bricks and other objects to use as weapons against the marshals.

One of the students, on his way back into the fray walked past Randy, bricks in hand.

"Where's your brick?" the student asked. "Grab one and come on."

"No way," Randy replied, dismissing the rioter with a wave of his arm.

About 11 p.m. a small military convoy approached the campus. The lead vehicle crashed through the barricade that the rioters had constructed to block the street, and the other vehicles followed through the breach. Some of the crowd along the roadway yelled curses and threw bricks at the soldiers and their vehicles.

"Go home!" they yelled. "You're traitors!"

Suddenly there was a rapid burst of gunfire from the direction of the Lyceum, and Randy heard someone standing not far from him yell, "I need help! He's been shot!"

With the other bystanders Randy rushed to the sound of the man's voice. He saw the man leaning helplessly over another man lying on the ground. Randy could see the bullet hole in the man's forehead. He couldn't tell if the man was still alive.

Randy had seen enough, sickened by the sight. He headed to his room.

He was halfway across the Circle, skirting the edge of the mob, when he came near four rioters wrestling with a photographer. One grabbed the man's camera and slammed it to the ground; the other three were dragging the photographer toward a clump of bushes near one of the dormitories. Although the area was unlighted, Randy could see that the victim was a large, thick-set individual with a heavy beard and a bushy mustache. None of the men seemed to notice Randy walking past, but he recognized one of the attackers. It was Billy Ray.

The university held classes the day after the riot, and Randy attended his, but many students chose to remain in their rooms as workers cleared the debris from the wake of the mob's actions and the tear gas slowly dissolved from the buildings and air. The National Guardsmen and other troops that President Kennedy had ordered to the campus to quell the riot were omnipresent, enforcing the lockdown to the campus, searching automobiles, and arresting unauthorized persons.

Randy learned that a second individual had died during the night's violence—a French news reporter who had apparently been murdered by an unidentified rioter. From the description of the reporter Randy believed he was the man he had seen being attacked by the four men, including Billy Ray. Had what he witnessed been the prelude to the man's execution? And had his friend been an accomplice in that act?

Randy's mother had called the morning after the riot to check on him. As soon as the campus lockdown was lifted, Randy drove home to assure his parents that he was all right. Randy quickly discovered that nothing had changed in his father's attitude. He was still spouting segregationist and racist invective.

"I see where folks sent Mr. Meredith and the Kennedys a powerful message," he said. "I thought about driving over there myself, but they didn't need my help. Ross has things well in hand. He'll take care of the problem."

For the first time in his life Randy felt compelled to confront his father. There was something about having experienced the insurrection—the mass hysteria and hatred exhibited by the mob, the physical abuse of the marshals and soldiers, the defection of the Highway Patrol—that angered and emboldened him.

"What do you folks want, Daddy? Another Civil War? Didn't you learn anything from the last one?"

"The other Civil War was just one battle," his father said. "The fight goes on. And we haven't lost it yet."

"So the old Lost Cause lives on," Randy said. "The white South has been in denial for a hundred years. We are Americans now, not Southerners."

"So you say," his father said. Then: "You know as well as I do that that n----r is not there to get an education. He just wants to stir up trouble."

"Actually, Daddy, truth be told, a lot of the students at Ole Miss are not there for an education. Some are there to play football, some of the males are there to screw co-eds, some of the females are there to find husbands. Education doesn't seem to be the top priority for many of the students I've met. I'm not even sure of my own motives anymore.

"But I do know this. James Meredith has honorably served his country in the military. And the nation he served is supposed to believe in equal justice and a Constitution that is color blind. He deserves the same rights and opportunities as you or me or anyone else. It's his state university as much as it is mine."

"Well, well. It didn't take you long to get brainwashed by those liberal professors we all know about. We'll get rid of them too, just as soon as we get rid of Meredith."

"And you believe the way to accomplish that is through vigilante action and attempted murder? Don't you believe in democracy?"

"Whatever it takes," his daddy said. "Our way of life is at stake."

A week after the riot Randy saw Billy Ray on campus and told him they needed to talk.

Randy and Billy Ray were not as close as they had been as young boys. They had remained friends throughout high school, and continuing into college, but over the years their relationship had cooled, become less intimate, more casual. More telling, Randy had observed elements in Billy Ray's character and behavior that bothered him. In middle school Billy Ray had frequently bullied younger students, and in high school he ran with a group of boys known for their wild and sometimes lawless antics. Since their childhood together, Randy had moved on to other friendships. They only occasionally saw each other on the Ole Miss campus.

"I saw you the night of the riot," Randy told Billy Ray. "You and three other guys were beating up that French reporter. My God, Billy Ray, somebody shot him!"

"It wasn't us," Billy Ray said. "We just roughed him up a bit. He was still alive when we left him."

"I can't believe you let yourself get caught up in all that mob violence," Randy said. "What were you thinking?"

"What I was thinking, and what I still think," Billy Ray said, "is that we can't let the federal government force its will upon us. Governor Barnett is right, integration is a matter for the states to decide."

"But the courts have said otherwise," Randy said. "They should be the ones to decide, don't you think, not savage vigilantes in the middle of the night. You sound like my dad, wanting to fight the Civil War all over again."

"Well, we need to fight it when they're trying to take away our way of life."

"Maybe some things in our way of life need to change. What about justice and

fairness and equal opportunity? Isn't
that what the Constitution is all about?"

"It's what northern liberals, and
apparently Southerners like you, say it's
all about. But schools belong to the
states, not the feds. It's covered in 'the
reserved powers,' in case you don't
remember."

"Yes," Randy replied, "but I believe all
of that is trumped by the individual
rights outlined in the Bill of Rights. I took
Mr. Rogers' Civics class too, you'll
recall."

Clearly they weren't going to agree on
Constitutional law, so Randy took a
different tack. "Do you ever think about
Syl?" he asked.

"Not really," Billy Ray said. "Why
should I?"

"I do," Randy said. "And when I see
Meredith on campus, I can't help but
wonder where Syl might be today. He

was smarter than either of us, you know."

"Well, maybe. But he was still a n----r."

"I never thought of him that way. And I don't think you did either. He was just a friend."

"That was a long time ago," Billy Ray said. "The problem with you, Randy, is that you never grew up. You still live in some make-believe world, where kids can pretend to be the Three Musketeers and play their fantasy games in the woods. You're in the real world now, and you have to fight for what you want—and to keep what you already have. Grow up."

With that, he turned and walked away.

Randy guessed—and certainly hoped—that Billy Ray had told the truth about the French reporter, but now he couldn't be quite so sure.

In the weeks and months that followed, Randy found himself a student at a University of Mississippi that had been drastically and irrevocably changed from what it formerly was. And would never be again. The reason for that change was the daily presence of James Meredith.

Throughout that school year Randy saw Meredith on campus every day or so—walking to class, eating in the cafeteria, sitting in the library, picking up his mail. In that regard he seemed just another student. But of course he wasn't. Everywhere he went there were one or more federal marshals at his side.

One day Randy stood behind Meredith as he collected his mail at the campus post office. It was delivered to him, as campus rumor reported that it always was, in a pasteboard box which, Randy could tell, contained dozens of letters, many of which, Randy surmised, were from well-wishers and supporters around the country but some of which, he felt sure, were from hatemongers and bigots communicating threats of reprisal or death. The segregationists on campus insisted that many of the letters contained money, and that it was primarily the desire for profit that led Meredith to the Ole Miss campus.

Randy had lived among blacks his entire life, playing with them, working in the fields with them, listening to their music. But previously he had never known an openly militant black who was fed up with the old system and refused to accept it any longer. Now just such a black had pushed his way into the same space that he occupied, demanding an equal share of that space.

And so it continued for the entire year. To Randy it seemed that his participation in the enforced integration of Ole Miss and the physical proximity of James Meredith throughout the 1962-63 school year affected almost everything he did, said, or thought. It was as though somehow the principle and condition of being Negro had wedged its way into his life and consciousness, indeed into his very soul, in a way that it never had before, despite his growing up in the South.

There was one other consequence of going to school with Meredith that Randy had not anticipated. Meredith's presence, sadly and unaccountably, brought back memories of Syl. How would he have turned out? Would he have attended college? Would he have been active in the civil rights movement? He was such an intelligent and good-natured kid. Surely he would have had a bright future. How sad that his life had come to such a premature and tragic end. Such goodness, such potential wasted. And why, Randy asked himself, could he not shake a sense of personal guilt about what had happened? Was there something about the accident that he had forgotten, something that his mind did not remember, perhaps did not want to remember? Whatever the case, Randy could not escape the troublesome feeling that he had perhaps in some way been partly responsible for the accident.

Randy hoped his father was wrong in saying that he was becoming brainwashed, but he did try to have an open mind about issues, and he was taking an American history class with the most liberal professor on campus. Dr. Lloyd Golden was not a native Mississippian, and being an outsider made his openly expressed critical views even more abominable to the state's conservatives, which included most of the white residents and nearly all of the politicians.

One day in class Dr. Golden drew a picture of a pyramid on the blackboard.

"This represents Southern history," he said, coloring the top portion of the pyramid with white chalk and filling in the bottom portion with x's.

"At the top of the pyramid you have the rich folks, mostly the owners of large plantations and others who profited off the institution of slavery. At the bottom, by far the majority, are the poor folks, both black and white.

"If you happened to be one of those rich folks at the apex of the pyramid and your privileged position was being threatened, you needed a strategy that would protect your place at the top of the heap. One strategy that worked was to get the blacks and poor whites at the bottom of the pyramid to view themselves as enemies and start fighting with each other. If they're obsessed with each other, maybe they won't pay as much attention to us.

"Logic would seem to dictate that the poor whites and blacks should have confederated and jointly opposed the economic system that shackled them both and deflected their attention from the power brokers at the top. But their hostility toward each other kept them from looking up. Thus the issue of race became a useful weapon to defend and perpetuate an unjust social and economic system.

"We no longer have slavery," Dr. Golden concluded, "but we still have the pyramid. And it's still undergirded by issues of race. Some say it's time to flatten the pyramid."

"That sounds like Marxism to me," one student interjected.

"Well, Marx wasn't wrong about everything, was he?" Golden replied.

Randy was also taking a literature class with Dr. Harriman, another professor who was known to be a liberal, but Randy signed up for the class because he had heard that Harriman was one of the finest lecturers on campus.

In that class Randy followed with interest the discussion of Robert Frost's poem "Mending Wall."

"Notice," Harriman said, "how Frost initially appears to play exactly fair in the poem, balancing the liberal 'Something there is that doesn't love a wall' with the conservative 'Good fences make good neighbors.'

"But then the imagery of the poem shifts in favor of the anti-traditionalist, as the narrator begins to question the need for walls and describes the reactionary as 'an old stone savage' who 'will not go behind his father's saying / And he likes having thought of it so well

/ He says again, 'Good fences make good neighbors.'"

After class Dr. Harriman often accompanied a few of his students for coffee at the Grill, where they continued their discussions. Randy occasionally joined the group, more to listen than to talk, and he found the sessions stimulating. He was becoming more aware of current events and the issues involved. While he was a staunch middle-of-the-roader, Randy had always liked ideas, and he was drawn to the sessions in which Harriman and some of his students questioned and challenged accepted views and the status quo.

In later years, as Randy looked back on these events, it seemed that the major impact that Meredith's presence at Ole Miss had on him was the contribution it made to his developing awareness of race and race relations. Never before or since had his reading, thinking, and formal education been so highly charged with relevance to existential experience. He knew that his view of race, democracy, and the world had been forever altered.

Those later years also brought Randy another realization, an ironic and disappointing one. While Meredith had been a catalyst for much that had happened in his life—much of it positive, Randy thought—he was not one of Randy's heroes. Randy soon concluded that his father was no doubt correct in his view that Meredith was not at Ole Miss to get an education. Or at least not merely so. He had a larger goal in mind—to change the traditional racial culture in Mississippi and open up more opportunities for its black citizens. This larger purpose became evident as Meredith continually scheduled news conferences to voice his concerns and complaints—not merely about his own situation but about the working conditions of black employees on campus and the status of Mississippi blacks in general. No wonder people concluded that his motive was political, not educational. Of course that's what they believed anyway; his actions just made it easier for them to do so.

More importantly, Randy came to disagree totally with the direction Meredith's life took after Ole Miss. Inexplicably, Meredith had become a Republican and a close ally of Senator Jesse Helms, a man with a racist past. Moreover, Meredith frequently expressed his opinion that the solution to the race problem in America was for blacks to return to Africa. Did he not know that Bilbo had said the same thing and had once introduced a bill to Congress that would implement such action? It seemed to Randy that the American justice system had worked for Meredith, had defended not only his life but his constitutional right to be free of discrimination and prejudice. And then Meredith had turned against that system, given up on it.

Still, give the man his due. He had shown great courage and taken action that changed both Mississippi and the nation for the better. And Randy wished that he had shown more open support for Meredith at Ole Miss. Among friends and acquaintances he voiced approval of Meredith's right to attend the university of his choice, and he exchanged greetings with Meredith when the two of them occasionally passed each other on campus; but, though ashamed later to admit it, he had never gone out of his way to engage him in an extended conversation or to befriend him in any way. But surely even Meredith must have recognized that the danger of his situation, in that time and place, discouraged all except the bravest or the most foolhardy from seeking his friendship.

Some whom Randy knew did reach out to Meredith—Golden and Harriman and some other liberal professors, the few students who dared to sit with Meredith in the school cafeteria, a small number of townsmen of Oxford. But they all paid a heavy price for their involvement—professors eventually censured or fired, students ostracized, townsmen receiving threatening phone calls and losing customers in their businesses.

Randy paid a price too, but his was more personal and private. He had met Wanda Joiner in a class they took together, and by the spring of his freshman year they were going steady. They had even spent an occasional night together at the Rebels Motel, a favorite spot for student trysts. Randy was persuaded that for the first time in his life he was in love.

Randy had driven to Greenwood to visit Wanda and her family several times. Her father owned a large Delta plantation, as well as some choice real estate in Greenwood. Randy hadn't decided yet what he wanted to do with his life, but if those plans didn't work out, whatever they might turn out to be, there would be excellent business opportunities with Mr. Joiner. Randy was thinking seriously about asking Wanda to marry him.

But those plans came to naught.

"You've changed," Wanda told him on a date that proved to be one of their last. "You're not as much fun as you used to be."

He tried to explain to her the inner struggle he was going through.

"I don't know how you can support that n----r being here," she said. "He and those like him are trying to destroy everything we hold dear."

Randy quickly became a great admirer of Dr. Harriman. He signed up for a second literature class with him. The son and grandson of Baptist preachers, Dr. Harriman had broken with the institutional church but still identified with a humanistic Jesus. A brilliant and entertaining lecturer, a legend on campus with his handsome looks, tweed jacket, and pipe ever at the ready, Dr. Harriman was a superstar with the students. And a gadfly for the school administration.

He and Dr. Golden both were board members of the Mississippi Alliance for Progress (MAP), a biracial group that worked to improve race relations throughout the state. Dr. Harriman invited Randy to attend the next meeting of the organization, which would be held in Jackson.

"Several students from Ole Miss, Tougaloo, and other schools will be attending," he told Randy. "I think you'll find the meeting interesting and educational."

On a Saturday morning in late April Randy climbed into Dr. Harriman's 1959 Buick Roadmaster, along with Dr. Golden and two other students, to begin the drive to the state capital. The group stopped in Weston to grab a bite to eat.

In the cafe a man at a table across the room recognized Dr. Golden.

"I didn't know they let n----r lovers eat in here," the man said to his companion, but clearly intending for Golden to hear.

Golden was well known across the state as an integrationist, but he was equally well known for his hot temper. He didn't take insults kindly.

"I've heard this town has more sons-of-bitches than any town in Mississippi," Golden said for all to hear. "I think I'll go introduce myself to one of them."

He rose from his chair and headed across the room.

Dr. Harriman quickly intervened and pushed Golden toward the door.

"You guys finish your meal and come on to the car," Harriman said to the students. "I'll come back in and pay," he told the waitress.

"Anytime you want," Golden hurled back at his offender as he left the room. The man made no further comment.

"Welcome to MAP," Harriman said to Randy when they were back on the road.

The meeting was held in the Student Union on the campus of Tougaloo College, an all-black school—according to Golden, one of the few places in Mississippi where integrated meetings could be held.

During the meeting various individuals, black and white, addressed the group—teachers, ministers, doctors, lawyers, business people. Randy sat in the back of the room and listened intently. He was also a bit awestruck. All of the blacks he had known growing up were sharecroppers, field hands, maids, cooks, and holders of menial jobs. And here he was listening to a group of sophisticated black professionals who spoke better English than he did.

Once over his shock, Randy began to listen to what the speakers were saying. They talked about job training and employment opportunities, voter registration, federal assistance, and integration. They praised the efforts of all involved but said more had to be done.

Not everything Randy heard, however, was friendly and conciliatory. A militant, angry, goateed young black man, whom Randy later learned was a member of the emerging Freedom Democrats, addressed the group: "Where are the field hands and cooks, the janitors and yard boys—the majority of the Negro population of this state—represented in this meeting?"

Dr. Harriman had said the meeting would be interesting and educational. And indeed it was, thought Randy.

Billy Ray's student career at Ole Miss proved just as eventful as Randy's, though at the opposite end of the political spectrum. Shortly after the Meredith riot, Billy Ray became involved in the demands to fire an Ole Miss art professor, Leonard Tapsky, who produced and exhibited several paintings based on the actions of the mob. In one of the paintings Tapsky created a montage of images associated with the riot. The painting displayed a replica of the Confederate flag on which were superimposed some of the vulgar and racist comments voiced by the segregationists—"Let's get this black bastard." "A good n----r is a dead n----r." "Back Ross." "Never." "Fuck the NAACP."

With the encouragement and support of the Mississippi Citizens' Council, Billy Ray teamed with two other students in filing a lawsuit against Tapsky for breaking the laws prohibiting obscenity and desecration of the Confederate flag. If convicted, Tapsky would face a substantial fine and up to six months in jail. And he would be fired. The charges were subsequently dismissed, but by then Billy Ray had become the darling of the segregationists across the state and the Daughters of the Confederacy.

Additionally, Billy Ray joined and became a leader in the Young Republicans Club, a group that supported segregation and states' rights. The Club joined the popular movement to get Golden, Harriman, and other liberal professors fired, and it sought to get the editor of the school paper, who argued for cooperation with the federal government and the U.S. Justice Department, dismissed from her position. The Club held rallies on campus and passed out flyers to the other students in support of their positions. Billy Ray was a principal spokesman for the group.

Fearful of the withdrawal of academic accreditation or, worse, the loss of federal funding, the university administration sought to walk the tightrope between the demands of the segregationists, including influential politicians in Jackson, on one hand and the expectations of the accreditation boards and the federal government on the other. To most objective observers, it seemed like a lose-lose situation. And it was a situation that drove Randy and Billy Ray further and further apart.

By the time he was a senior, Randy's liberalization—or, as he later phrased it, his liberation—was complete. Meredith had graduated, but additional African Americans had enrolled at Ole Miss, and, though pockets of resistance still existed on campus—as when a small group of students protested during an integrated literary event organized and hosted by Professor Harriman—by and large the university, and most of its students, were settling into an acceptance of the new order of things.

Off campus, however, the old order still ruled, and reactionaries continued to engage in their nefarious practices. The murders of Medgar Evers and the three civil rights activists—Goodman, Schwerner, and Chaney—in Neshoba County had pushed Randy solidly and irreversibly into the liberal camp. He traveled to Jackson to participate in the Woolworth's sit-in organized by Ed King, the Tougaloo College chaplain. He rode with a busload of sympathizers to Washington D.C. to participate in the march and hear Martin Luther King speak. By now he had concluded that he wanted to go to law school and perhaps become a civil rights lawyer.

His father's attitude had not changed and, if anything, had become even more rigid. For this reason, as his years at Ole Miss drew to a close, Randy didn't go back home very often. But with graduation now only a few weeks away, he decided he must make a visit. He felt he owed it to his parents to explain his future plans.

He still planned to go to law school, but he was thinking now that maybe it should be out of state, possibly somewhere up north. He wondered if perhaps he should leave Mississippi for a while, gain a broader perspective. But telling his parents about his decision would be hard.

"What's wrong with you?" his father interrupted when Randy had just begun. "What in the hell is happening to you?"

"John, be patient," his mother said. "Let him finish."

"A lot has happened to cause me to question who I am, what I believe in, what my values are," Randy said. "Some of that has to do with race, but there are other issues as well. I just think I need some time away from here to sort out a few things. To see how things might look from another part of the world."

"Where do you get such crazy ideas?" his father asked.

"Well," Randy laughed. "Some of it comes from that woman sitting there beside you. She's always been more kind, gentle, and understanding than you. I guess I've always been a mama's boy. She's taught me a lot."

His father started to speak, but then didn't.

Randy continued. "Maybe too I paid more attention than you did to that New Testament they taught us in Sunday School. Especially those passages about love and that story of the Good Samaritan. Jesus was black, you know."

"He was not!" his father snapped.

"Well, he was closer to black than white. Let's just say colored."

Randy knew now that he and his father would never come to an agreement about race. He thought back to the comment his dad had once made about giving blacks an inch and they'd take a mile. Ironically, Randy now realized, his father had expressed a truth in the comment. But that truth lay with him, Randy, not with blacks. Until the last couple of years he had been progressing through life by inches; now he found himself beginning a journey that would be marked by miles.

That journey would take him initially to the University of Missouri law school and subsequently to a successful career with a civil rights law firm in St. Louis, as well as a childless marriage and divorce. Then, after more than two decades had passed, it would bring him back to his roots in Mississippi.

THREE

Randy had only a few more days of vacation left. He had not intended to stay in Blyden this long; now he was thinking of calling his law office and extending his time away even longer. He always tried to keep his calendar relatively free right after vacation so he could ease back into the work. So there was no urgent need for his immediate return. He still had not been able to locate Syl's parents, but he planned to continue the effort.

One afternoon when Randy returned to his motel, the desk clerk informed him that he had received a phone call with a request that the call be returned. The clerk handed him the number.

Randy went to his room and dialed the number. A woman answered the call.

"I'm Randy Morris. You called me earlier."

"Yes, I'm Margaret White, Billy Ray's widow. I'd like to talk with you sometime if it's convenient."

Thus it developed that Randy sat with Margaret White for an hour in a McDonald's restaurant in Blyden and talked about the individual who had been so important in both of their lives. Randy found Margaret to be quite attractive—tall, elegant, erudite, with smoky brown eyes and dark hair just beginning to show traces of gray.

"I'm sorry for your loss. My condolences," Randy began.

"Thank you," Margaret said. "It was such a shock to us all. He was healthy one day and gone the next."

"Several people have told me about all the good things he did for Blyden and this part of the state. I know you're proud of that."

"Yes, he was a dedicated public servant," Margaret said. "But he was also a very troubled individual, and apparently you had something to do with that. Can you explain it to me?"

"I'm not sure I can," Randy said. "We were boyhood pals, really close, but we grew distant as the years passed. Our differing political views came between us. I've come to regret that. Perhaps he did too."

"Yes, I think so. He often talked about you, and about that black kid y'all played with—what was his name?"

"Slyvester Johnson, Syl."

"Yes. It was as though he remembered those boyhood years as a special time of innocence that he lost and could never recover."

"I did too. Still do. I think Freud had a lot to say about that. And a host of writers, like Blake and Wordsworth and Dickens. The Book of Genesis, too, for that matter. That's life, I suppose."

"I know. But for Billy Ray, it seemed more complicated and troubling than for most people. He always saw it as some kind of betrayal. I think it was partly because of the work he did. Politicians have to be pragmatists. Sometimes they have to rein in their principles and preferences to get the desired results— to get reelected, to get a bill passed, to persuade others to agree."

"The end justifies the means," Randy said. "It's an old argument, probably justified in some instances. It seems to me that culpability, or credit, is always a matter of degree."

"People say it was the pressure of his work that caused the heart attack," Margaret said. "But I don't think so. I think it was more personal. He was such a divided soul.”

She sighed, and then after a long pause, continued.

“I think something happened at Ole Miss that really bothered him. He wouldn’t talk to me about it, but he was obsessed by the Meredith event. He read Meredith’s book and everything he could find about the riot. I didn’t know him then. We met after he was elected to the legislature. You were with him at Ole Miss. What do you recall?”

“Billy Ray was a part of the mob that opposed Meredith’s enrollment. How much of the violence he participated in I don’t know. Perhaps he came to regret his actions of that night. We all make mistakes that later haunt us.”

“He wasn’t a white supremacist or a racist—at least not after I came to know him. He had to associate and cooperate with such people to get his political agenda accomplished, but he was not a bad person. And a lot of what he did in Jackson improved the lives of blacks."

Randy could not tell if she actually believed this, or if she were just trying to persuade herself that it was true.

"He envied you," Margaret said. "He followed your career. He thought you were so decent and principled."

"Billy Ray was principled as well. He believed the federal government had overstepped its authority at Ole Miss. I quarreled with his means of protest, but I never doubted his sincerity. And sometimes, as the years passed, I came to agree with him on that issue."

"Consider yourself fortunate that you didn't enter politics," Margaret said. "That life is impossible, I think, without a considerable amount of hypocrisy. At least if you want to stay in office."

Her emotions overwhelming her, she began to weep. Then, regaining control, she said, "Here's an irony you'll find interesting. Our son Chris is more like you than Billy Ray. They say the apple doesn't fall far from the tree, but in this case it did."

"Well, I know something about that. I turned out quite different from my dad as well. But I still loved my dad."

Randy followed Roger Magee's suggestion and gave Mary Jo Abbott a call. He invited her to have dinner with him and she accepted. For old time's sake, they agreed.

They drove to Tupelo, since it was the closest town with a nice restaurant. It was twenty miles from Blyden, and they traveled on the "Billy Ray White Memorial Highway."

Mary Jo was still just as beautiful as she was in high school—petite, shapely, with blonde hair and blue eyes, an engaging personality, and a bright smile.

They went to an Italian restaurant and ordered chicken tetrazzini. They had a glass of wine with the meal.

"You couldn't do this when we grew up," Randy laughed, as he touched his glass to Mary Jo's. "Now, I hear, even Baptists can drink in front of one another."

As they ate, they reminisced about their school days together, and the years after.

"Do you remember Tommy Watson, the bookworm who couldn't get a date?" Mary Jo asked. "He wound up as a NASA engineer in Houston. I heard he was one of the scientists who figured out how to get the Apollo 13 astronauts back from the moon. And he did finally get a date. He's married with three kids."

"And Janice Adams?" Randy said. "She's quite an artist. She teaches at SMU. I have a couple of her paintings."

"And Billy Ray," Mary Jo said. "I think he would have become governor had he lived. He certainly knew how to dole out political favors. You've seen the beltway around Blyden, I'm sure. A town of 3,000 with a beltway. I think one of Billy Ray's supporters must have been in the concrete business."

Then their talk turned to personal matters.

Mary Jo went to the University of Alabama, studied accounting, married an architect, lived in Atlanta, had two kids.

"But I always came back here for visits," she said. "My sister still lives here. She never left. How about you?"

"This is my first time back here in over twenty years. I didn't think I'd ever come back."

Randy explained how, given his experiences at Ole Miss and his conflict with his dad, he felt he needed to get away from Mississippi. After law school at the University of Missouri, he wound up at a law firm in St. Louis. He was now a senior partner in the firm.

"Funny thing about that," he said. "Missouri was a slave state, and St. Louis is still very much a Southern city. I guess I didn't go far enough north."

"One of your cases made the national news," Mary Jo said. "We heard about that one down here."

"Yes, it was a case involving discrimination in a newly-built apartment complex in one of the suburbs. Minorities were being discriminated against. We won the case and it became something of a precedent for similar cases around the country."

"And now, like me, you're divorced. Why?"

"Beverly and I were married ten years. Bottom line is that she wanted kids and I didn't. My dad and I didn't have a very good relationship, and I wasn't sure I could do any better. The ironic thing is that after I gave in to Beverly, it turned out we couldn't have kids. Then she wanted to adopt and I didn't. Things kinda fell apart after that."

"What's your story?" Randy asked.

"I discovered that Richard had found someone else. In fact, several someone elses. I got tired of being second-choice. I had a job so I could be self-supporting. The kids were grown and out on their own. So I asked for a divorce. That was four years ago."

"And why did you come back here?"

"Atlanta is a terrible place to live these days. The traffic is horrendous. Plus too many bad memories. And accountants can get work anywhere."

"Do you have kids?" Randy asked.

"Yes, a boy and a girl. And three grandsons."

Driving back to Blyden, Randy said, "This has been a fun evening. Let's do it again."

"Sure," Mary Jo said.

"I hear you had a date with Mary Jo," Roger said during the dinner he had invited Randy to share with him and his wife Jennie.

"Just a visit," Randy said, "reliving old times."

"How'd it go?" Roger asked.

"It was fun," Randy said. "She's still the same girl we all loved in high school."

"Guess you'll be going back to St. Louis soon," Roger said.

"Yes, duty calls," Randy said.

"It's sure been good seeing you again. Wish you would come more often."

"Maybe I will," Randy said.

"In fact," Roger added, "why don't you just consider coming on back here to live. Mississippi is changing, despite what most people think. We now have more elected black officials than any state in the union."

"All Roger has talked about lately is your being back in town," Jennie said. "He'd love to have you back."

"Well, Roger has always had an exaggerated opinion of me. I'd hate to come back and ruin that."

"I'm just thinking we could use you around here," Roger said. "You might even get me to come out of the closet and join you in your crusade."

"How about another helping of the Swiss steak?" Jennie asked.

"No, thanks," Randy said. "I don't think I could eat another bite. The whole meal was delicious. I can see why Roger is as healthy as he is. You are a wonderful cook. And I appreciate the invitation to dinner. I don't get many home-cooked meals, except those I cook for myself. And I'm not a very good cook."

"All the more reason to come back home," Roger said. "There's no food as good as Southern cooking."

They left the table and went into the den.

"How are things out at New Harmony?" Roger asked.

"Fine, I guess. Nothing's the same, of course. They even moved part of the road when they paved it. I've been spending some time at the farm. Not sure why I've kept it."

"There's always a reason," Roger said. "I'm sure you'll figure it out." Then, after a pause: "Any interesting cases coming up when you get back to St. Louis?"

"Not really. For years civil rights cases dealt largely with discrimination against blacks. Now they're just as likely to deal with women, especially on the abortion issue, or with gays. With the election coming up, there will be questions about voting rights."

"How will the election go, do you think?" Roger asked.

"Clinton has a good chance to win, I think," Randy said. "He should carry Missouri, since he's from a neighboring state."

"Bush will probably hold Mississippi," Roger said. "The big question is Perot, whether he will run or not. He has really cut into Bush's numbers in the early polling."

"Politics has become nastier and nastier," Randy said. "More and more divisive. Seems like now it's all about me and my party. Don't we have any statesmen anymore? Now we just have politicians."

"That's true," Roger said. "But you know, that was the thing about Billy Ray. I didn't agree with his positions on a lot of issues, but he could work across the aisle and get things done. He accomplished quite a lot to benefit this area."

"His wife told me the same thing. I'm glad to hear it."

"Well, you're right about Washington. The legacy of Watergate, I think," Roger said. "You did it to me, now it's payback time. It's like when we kids used to get caught fighting and our excuse was always, 'He started it.' I think it will only get worse."

He had put off making this visit as long as he could. But he knew that, sooner or later, he had to make it.

Billy Ray was buried in the cemetery at the New Harmony Baptist Church, the same cemetery where Randy's parents lay. The grave was in the White family plot, together with those for Billy Ray's grandparents, father, and infant sister.

Randy stood at the grave for quite a while, reflecting on the mystery of how two individuals who came out of the same place and circumstances could wind up at opposite poles of thought and action. And how such good friends could become, in effect, enemies. But it happened all too frequently. And you saw it in the social fabric and body politic as well. It was as though some element were missing in the heart of man.

It was late afternoon, and the sky had been overcast all day. Now the wind was picking up, and rain was on the way. So Randy broke off his ruminations and headed back to the car.

Then the wind spoke.

"I didn't think you were ever coming to see me. You didn't come to the funeral."

"I'm sorry," Randy said. "No one called me. We hadn't communicated for a long time, you know."

"You left me," the wind said.

"I thought you left me. I didn't agree with the person you became."

"But we were friends. That should have counted for more."

"There were principles involved," Randy said.

"What good are principles if they divide friends and destroy relationships? Compromise is necessary. Reconciliation of opposites. Sometimes even forgiveness. I learned that in politics. You haven't learned it yet."

"I didn't see any evidence of your willingness to compromise at Ole Miss," Randy said.

The wind was picking up, building to a roar, whipping the trees violently.

"I made mistakes," the wind said. "You did too. I tried to atone for mine. You need to atone for yours."

"And you're going to tell me what mine were?"

"You must discover that for yourself. But remember what they taught us about macrocosm and microcosm. You will never find peace and order and harmony in the larger world until you find them within yourself. Life involves conflict. But you must avoid the extremes. You must find a balance. You see things more clearly from this side."

The storm quickly subsided, a brief interruption in an otherwise calm day, settling into a gentle rain.

"Go see Syl," the wind said, as it passed on.

Go see Syl, the wind said.

So Randy went once again to the site of the accident.

He went first to where the time capsule was buried and dug up the box. He removed Syl's rabbit foot and put it in his pocket. Then he returned the box to the ground and walked on.

Had he accurately remembered all the details of what happened? It had been a long time ago, and memory often blurs or distorts events, even forgets. And for a long time now Randy had been troubled by the recurring thought that maybe he had forgotten something. He had heard about trauma victims who suppress terrible experiences from their past as a coping mechanism—buried them deeply in their subconscious in order not to have to confront them. Could that possibly be what he had done?

Go see Syl, the wind said.

Now Randy stood in the exact spot where he had stood when he and Billy Ray pushed the cart down the hill with Syl aboard. He willed his mind to see again every single detail—the red wagon wheels, the silver spokes of the bicycle wheels, the uneven boards hammered together to make the bed, the baling wire holding the contraption together. He saw the whitish clay dirt packed down and smoothed to make the runway. He saw the steep incline sloping toward the bottom of the hill. He saw Syl's huge smile as he climbed onto the cart and took his seat.

And then he saw something else— something he hadn't remembered before, though he had relived the event hundreds of times. It was as though his memory had been swimming for a long time under water, and then, lungs bursting, broke to the surface. He noticed that the baling wire holding the left front wheel in place had worked loose. It appeared to be still attached to the wheel, but it was clearly failing.

Randy fell back in shock, stunned by his discovery. Was the loose wire what caused the wheel to come off the axle? If so, why didn't Randy call the problem to Syl's and Billy Ray's attention and halt the run? Did he not realize the danger to Syl that the threat posed? Or did he tell himself that Syl would not be hurt even if the cart crashed? Or was there something deeper and more sinister in his psyche, a subconscious desire to witness the wreck—like the intoxicating thrill that human beings derive from watching an automobile wreck or a plane crash or a building burn or men destroying other men in battle?

Whatever the case, Randy now reacted with horror at the recognition and realization that he could possibly have been to blame for Syl's death. No wonder he had hidden that fact from himself all these years.

Randy still had found no one who knew where Syl's parents might be living. The only clue was Mr. Martin's remark that they might have moved to Corinth. So he drove to Corinth and resumed his search there.

He first stopped at a convenience store and borrowed its phone book. But no Robert or Clara Johnson was listed.

He next went to the post office but was told that, because of privacy issues, personal addresses could not be given out.

"You might try the utilities company, Alcorn Power and Light, just down the street," the mail clerk said. "If they pay a light bill, there would be a record."

And, after a generous tip to the receptionist, there was. The address was just west of town, off Highway 72.

Clara Johnson came to the door. Randy recognized her immediately, though she was elderly and stooped and walked with a cane. But her face was alert and animated, and her voice was strong.

"I'm Randy Morris, Mrs. Johnson. You may remember that Syl and I used to be playmates."

"Lordy mercy," she said. "Randy Morris. Come right in here, boy."

The house was small and cramped, with the smell that often accompanies old age, medications, and poor ventilation.

She led him into the small living room and directed him to a couch with worn and frayed cushions. She sat down beside him and took his hand. She was slowly shaking her head, as though in disbelief, and smiling.

"Where you been all these years?" she asked.

"I live in St. Louis. I've been spending a few days in Blyden and New Harmony. I had a hard time finding you."

"Well, I'm so glad you did. Robert is taking his rest right now, but I'll go get him in a minute. I know he'll want to see you."

"Do you remember that Syl, Billy Ray White, and I used to play together when we were little boys?"

"Of course I remember. We couldn't keep Sylvester at home. He was always running off to the woods with you boys."

"I told you at the time but I want to tell you again how sorry I am about Syl's passing."

"It was merciful, the condition he was in. The doctors told us he probably wouldn't live long since he was totally paralyzed. And how could we take care of him? The Lord knew it was best to take him on home."

"Billy Ray has died too," Randy said. "Did you know that?"

"Yes, he was our representative. He helped us get our Medicaid. He was a good man."

"I wanted to ask if I could help you in any way," Randy said. "Do you need anything? Do you have anybody who helps you?"

"Our oldest daughter, Dustina, lives in Corinth. She's one of the cooks at the high school. She checks on us regular. She drives us to the doctor and runs errands for us. We make it fine."

She released his hand and stood up.

"Let me go see if Robert is awake."

She was gone for several minutes, and when she returned she was pushing Robert in a wheelchair.

"Look who's come to see us," Clara said to Robert. "Randy Morris. We lived on his daddy's place, you remember?"

Robert reached out his hand weakly to Randy, but the recognition seemed doubtful.

"He's forgetful," Clara said. "We're not as young as we used to be."

"It's good to see you again, Mr. Johnson. It's been a long time," Randy said.

"Thank you," Robert said. He seemed distracted, disoriented. Clearly his mind was somewhere else.

Randy had intended to tell them about his role in the accident. But now he thought, what would be the point? Robert wouldn't understand, and it would just open up fresh wounds for Clara.

Instead he reached for his billfold and took out one of his business cards and handed it to Clara.

"I want you to give this to Dustina. I'm going back to St. Louis in a couple of days, and I want her to call me collect so I can talk with her. And I want her to call me anytime you need help."

"Thank you," Clara said. "You're very kind."

As he walked to the door, she said, "You three boys were really close, weren't you. Almost like brothers."

"Yes, we were," Randy said.

Driving back to Blyden, he reflected on Clara's last words. All the years he thought it had been the Meredith incident and his years at Ole Miss that had set his life on its trajectory. But now he realized it had started much earlier— with his boyhood friendship with Syl and Billy Ray.

Randy knows that it is time for him to go back to St. Louis. He has been away too long. There is work there that must be done. So he drives out to the old home place and takes one more stroll around the yard and through the trees. This is a good place, he tells himself, a place where once he was happy and carefree and yet innocent of all the complications and hurt and confusion that the world would hurl at him in the years to come. He could never have that again, he knows, but perhaps there is another kind of peace and contentment that can be known later in life.

He returns to the car and stands beside it for a moment, casting his gaze once more around the farm. He sees a new house standing where the one he remembers from his childhood once stood. He sees a man and a woman, past middle age but not yet old, living in the house. They sit together in a swing on the front porch as the twilight settles on the close of day, listening to the choiring of the crickets and tree frogs and watching the lightning bugs flaming the air. Looking toward the woods, they see three young boys coming home from an afternoon of play, laughing and talking, completely oblivious to everything but themselves, happy to be in each other's company.

Yes, this is a good place, Randy thinks. It once was, and it can be again.

He climbs into his car and drives away. But he knows he will return, and soon.